Dirty Bertie

SPIDER!

DAVID ROBERTS WRITTEN BY ALAN MACDONALD

Stripes

Collect all the
Dirty Bertie books!

Dirty Bertie

SPIDER!

For Corban McBride and Skye Russell ~ D R
For Grace Styles ~ A M

STRIPES PUBLISHING LTD
An imprint of the Little Tiger Group
1 Coda Studios, 189 Munster Road,
London SW6 6AW

A paperback original
First published in Great Britain in 2019

Characters created by David Roberts
Text copyright © Alan MacDonald, 2019
Illustrations copyright © David Roberts, 2019

ISBN: 978-1-84715-946-5

Printed and bound in the UK.

10 9 8 7 6 5 4 3 2 1

Contents

CHAPTER 1

"YAAAARGHHH!"

Mum's scream made Bertie drop his spoon in his Wheeto Flakes. He rushed upstairs to find his family on the landing.

Mum was standing outside the bathroom wrapped in a towel.

"There's a spider in the bath!" she cried.

"Is that all?" Dad laughed. "I thought it

was something serious!"

"You haven't seen the spider," said Mum.

Suzy shuddered. "UGH! I hate spiders."

"Can I see it?" begged Bertie.

"No, you keep out of the way, Bertie, I'll deal with this," said Dad.

He marched into the bathroom. A moment later he marched back out again, looking shaken.

Dirty Bertie

"That's a *really* big spider," he admitted.

"I told you," said Mum. "Well, aren't you going to do something?"

"Yes, you can't just leave it in the bath," said Suzy.

"Okay, okay, I'm working on it," replied Dad. It wasn't that he was scared of spiders, he just wasn't very keen on picking them up.

"I can catch it for you!" cried Bertie.

Mum and Dad looked at each other. Clearly neither of them were about to go back in and tackle the spider.

"Well, okay," sighed Dad. "But for goodness' sake don't let it escape."

Bertie hurried off to fetch his school lunch box. It was the perfect size for a spider trap. He crept into the bathroom on tiptoe.

Dirty Bertie

"WOAH! It's massive!" he cried.

"Just get rid of it," groaned Mum. "And *hurry up, I'm freezing to death!*"

The spider was sitting halfway up the bath. It was dark, hairy and almost as big as Bertie's hand.

Bertie wasn't scared of spiders though, and this one was a real whopper. Maybe it was a rare species – a King Kong spider or a giant vampire spider perhaps?

Bertie got into the bath with his lunch box at the ready.

"It's okay, Mr Spider, I won't hurt you," he whispered.

SLAM! He brought down the box. The spider made a run for it but Bertie

Dirty Bertie

was too quick for him.

"GOT YOU!" he cried, jamming on the lid.

His family were waiting outside.

"Well? Did you get it?" asked Suzy.

"Yes," said Bertie, holding up the box. "Look, he's a monster!"

Dirty Bertie

"EWWW!" yelled Suzy.

"Take it away!" shrieked Mum.

Bertie couldn't see what all the fuss was about. It was only a spider – anyone would think it was a man-eating python or something!

"Please, just get rid of it," said Dad.

"Can't I keep it?" asked Bertie.

"NO!" cried everyone at once.

"Just for a few days?" pleaded Bertie. "I've never had a pet spider."

"Absolutely not," said Mum. "And before you get any ideas, don't try hiding it in your room."

"Let it go in the garden," said Dad. "And then you better get off to school."

Bertie sighed. You'd think his parents would be pleased he wanted to look after a poor homeless spider. Weren't

Dirty Bertie

they always saying he should be kind to all living creatures?

He took the lunch box out to the front garden and removed the lid.

"Sorry, Mr Spider, I'm not allowed to keep you," he sighed.

The spider clung to the bottom of the box.

Dirty Bertie

It was a pity no one at school would ever see him, thought Bertie. Darren and Eugene would be dead impressed. Know-All Nick would probably faint with fright. It was no use though, his mean parents refused to have the spider in the house. But hang on a moment, they hadn't said anything about *other* houses. Bertie smiled and replaced the lid. All he needed was someone to look after his spider for a little while — and luckily he knew just the person.

CHAPTER 2

DING DONG!

Bertie rang Gran's doorbell. He was late for school but this wouldn't take a minute.

Gran answered the door wearing her dressing gown.

"Bertie, what are you doing here?" she asked. "Is something the matter?"

"No, I just wanted to ask you something," replied Bertie.

"Can't it wait?" sighed Gran. "I've only just got up."

"It's sort of urgent," said Bertie. "Can you look after something for me?"

He held out the plastic lunch box. The lid had rows of tiny air holes, which Bertie had made with a fork. Gran could see a dark something moving inside.

"What is it?" she asked. "It's not a mouse?"

"Of course not, it's my pet spider," said Bertie. "I'm calling him Tickler."

"Let's have a look then," said Gran. She took the box a little cautiously and lifted the lid.

"WAAAH!" She dropped it quickly. "Are you trying to scare me to death?"

Bertie picked up the box and scooped Tickler inside.

"I found him in the bath," he explained. "Or actually Mum found him but she won't let me keep him."

"I'm not surprised," said Gran.

"So anyway, can you look after him for a bit?" asked Bertie.

17

"Not likely!" said Gran. "I'm not having that thing in the house. It'll give me nightmares. Why can't you have a pet hamster like other children?"

"Mum says Whiffer is enough trouble," replied Bertie.

"Well, I'm sorry, but I can't help you," said Gran. "If you want my advice, let that spider go. Now, aren't you late for school?"

Bertie put the lunch box back in his bag and trailed off down the road.

At the school gates he caught up with Darren and Eugene.

"What happened to you?" asked Eugene.

"Sorry, I had to ask my gran about something," explained Bertie. "But wait till you see what I've got."

He brought out the lunch box and carefully lifted the lid.

Darren and Eugene stared boggle-eyed.

"WOAH! That's *ginormous*!" cried Darren.

"Where did you get him?" asked Eugene.

"He was sitting in the bath," replied Bertie. "He's called Tickler."

"Maybe he's a tarantula?" suggested Darren. "They're the biggest spiders in the universe!"

"And the deadliest," added Eugene. "Aren't tarantulas meant to be poisonous?"

"Probably," said Bertie. "I've never had one. Do you think he *is* a tarantula?"

They all stared at Tickler – who seemed quite harmless for a deadly spider. All the same, owning a pet tarantula would be brilliant, thought Bertie. His classmates would have to treat him with more respect. Know-All Nick wouldn't dare call him "bogey nose" ever again.

"Wait, you're not bringing him to school, are you?" said Eugene.

"Why not?" asked Bertie.

Dirty Bertie

"Because Miss Boot will go crackers if she sees him."

"She won't see him," replied Bertie.

"Well, be careful," warned Darren. "If he *is* a tarantula, he better not escape."

"Relax," said Bertie. "It's all under control."

Obviously he wasn't going to let a giant tarantula loose in school – he wasn't *that* stupid!

CHAPTER 3

During morning lessons, Bertie kept
the lunch box under his desk where he
could keep an eye on Tickler. Eugene
had found *The Bumper Book of Bugs* on
the class bookshelf, which had a double
page on spiders. It made interesting
reading. Bertie had no idea tarantulas
were so huge and scary.

TARANTULA
(HAIRIUS BEASTUS)

Largest known spider, which can grow as big as your dinner plate.

Diet:
grasshoppers, beetles and other spiders

Yikes! thought Bertie. The spider in the picture wasn't something you'd want crawling up your leg. Tickler wasn't that big but maybe he was still a baby?

At break time, Bertie and his friends headed for a bench in the playground. Bertie took out his lunch box.

23

"Don't let him out!" cried Eugene in alarm.

"I'm not," said Bertie. "I'm just checking he's all right."

"Has he eaten anything?" asked Darren.

Bertie shook his head. He'd left Tickler a piece of cheese but it was still untouched. It was a pity he didn't have any grasshoppers or beetles.

"What are you looking at?"

Bertie looked up to see Royston Rich, the biggest boaster in the class. He snapped the lid back on the box.

"If you must know it's a spider," he said. "He's called Tickler and he's a tarantula."

"OH, HA HA!" scoffed Royston. "As if you'd have a tarantula! I don't think so!"

"You haven't seen him," said Darren. "He's almost as big as your head."

Dirty Bertie

Royston folded his arms. "Prove it. Let me see," he demanded.

Bertie considered it. A pet tarantula could turn out to be very useful.

"I can't let you see him for free," he said. "What have you got?"

Royston rolled his eyes. He reached into his bag and handed over a fudge bar.

Bertie put it in his pocket. Checking that no teachers were around, he lifted the lid.

"WOAH!" squawked Royston. "That's a monster!"

"Told you," said Bertie. "He's a tarantula."

"How do you know?" asked Royston.

"We read it in a book," said Darren.

Bertie decided they should have some fun with Royston.

"Did you know that tarantulas can bite?" he asked.

"C-can they?" gulped Royston.

"Oh yes, if a tarantula bites you, your face turns yellow and all your teeth fall out," said Bertie.

Royston took a step back. "I ... um ... better be going," he said, hurrying off.

"You made that up," said Eugene.

"It wasn't in the book."

"I know," grinned Bertie, "but Royston doesn't."

This was brilliant. He could make up anything he liked and everyone would believe it.

Before long, word spread around the playground and a queue formed. Bertie was offered sweets and crisps to see the deadly tarantula.

"So where's this scary spider, then?"

Bertie smiled. He might have guessed Know-All Nick would poke his nose in sooner or later.

"He's in the box," said Bertie.

"I bet it's not a tarantula at all," sneered Nick. "It's probably just a dopey daddy-long-legs."

"It's a tarantula," said Bertie.

"Liar, liar, pants on fire!" chanted Nick.

Dirty Bertie

Bertie scowled. "Look, smelly-pants, do you want to see him or not?" he demanded.

Nick pulled a face and handed over half a jelly snake. Bertie added it to his growing pile of goodies.

"You have to come close," said Bertie. "But be careful, he might jump on you."

Bertie lifted the lid as Nick peered inside.

"G-golly!" gulped Nick. "That's a big one!"

"Tarantulas are the biggest and the deadliest," said Bertie.

Nick bent his head a little closer.

"He's not moving," he said. "Are you sure he's alive?"

"Oh, he's alive all right," said Bertie.

He tapped the box and Tickler suddenly scuttled to the other end.

"YEEAAAARGHHH!" wailed Nick, leaping back in fright. "You did that on purpose! I'm telling Miss Boot!"

"You better not," warned Bertie. "Or I might put a tarantula down your trousers."

"You wouldn't!" gasped Nick.

"Try me," said Bertie. "Do you know what happens when you're bitten by a tarantula?"

Nick didn't but he wasn't waiting to find out. He ran off as fast as he could.

Bertie took a bite of the jelly snake. This was a gold mine, he thought. With a few more Ticklers he could open a spider zoo and make a fortune!

CHAPTER 4

Back in class, everyone settled into their
seats. Bertie noticed that Trevor and
Amanda had moved further away from
him. Clearly they weren't too keen on
sharing the classroom with a tarantula.
While Miss Boot wrote maths questions
for the class, Bertie took the chance to
check on Tickler.

Dirty Bertie

HELP! OH PANTS! OH NO! He'd escaped!

Bertie emptied out his bag on the floor. No Tickler.

"What are you doing?" asked Eugene.

"I can't find Tickler!" hissed Bertie.

"What? You're joking!"

"No! He's not in his box!" muttered Bertie.

Bertie looked under his chair with growing panic. It was one thing scaring his classmates – it was another having a tarantula loose in the classroom. What if Tickler crawled up somebody's leg? What if he actually bit them? They might really turn yellow or even drop dead on the spot! Miss Boot would guess he was to blame. Who else would bring a deadly spider into school?

Dirty Bertie

As Miss Boot droned on, Bertie slid down under his desk. There was no sign of Tickler. Bertie inched forwards on his hands and knees, searching the floor.

"Here, Tickler! Where are you?" he whispered.

"BERTIE!" boomed Miss Boot.

Bertie froze.

Now he was for it.

Dirty Bertie

"Come out from there!" ordered
Miss Boot.

Bertie struggled to his feet.

"WELL?" thundered Miss Boot.
"What were you doing?"

"Nothing," mumbled Bertie. "I just
lost something."

"Speak up!" snapped Miss Boot.
"What have you lost?"

"My um ... my pet spider," admitted
Bertie.

The class gasped.

"IT'S A GIANT TARANTULA! WE'RE
ALL GOING TO DIE!" wailed Nick.

Panic swept through the class as
children screamed and leaped to their
feet. They fled to Miss Boot, clinging
to her for protection. Know-All Nick
climbed on to a desk and tried to

Dirty Bertie

escape through the window. Bertie
hadn't seen chaos like this since the
time Whiffer did something in Royston's
swimming pool.

"QUIET!" thundered Miss Boot.
"Everyone calm down and look on
the floor."

Dirty Bertie

Out of the corner of his eye, Bertie saw something scuttle out from a desk. Tickler! Miss Boot saw him too. Cutting him off, she brought her hand down on the spider. The class held their breath. They waited for her to scream, turn yellow and drop dead on the spot. But Miss Boot did none of these things. She lifted Tickler up and dropped him into a plastic cup on her desk.

"For your information, Bertie, this is NOT a tarantula," she said. "Tarantulas are much bigger and they live in the rainforest. This is just a common house spider. It couldn't bite you if it tried."

"You lied!" bleated Nick. "I gave you half my jelly snake."

"And I gave you my fudge bar," said Royston.

Dirty Bertie

"Did you indeed?" said Miss Boot. "Well, I'm sure Bertie will be only too happy to return anything he took. But first I have a job for him. Come here, Bertie."

Bertie trailed out to the front.

"Take this horrid creature and get rid of it," ordered Miss Boot. "I never ever want to see it in school again."

Bertie headed down the corridor with Tickler back in his box. This time the spider would have to go for good… Or would he? At the main door Bertie paused and turned round. An idea had come to him. There was one place in school Miss Boot would never look for Tickler. And better still, Bertie would be able to visit him whenever he liked.

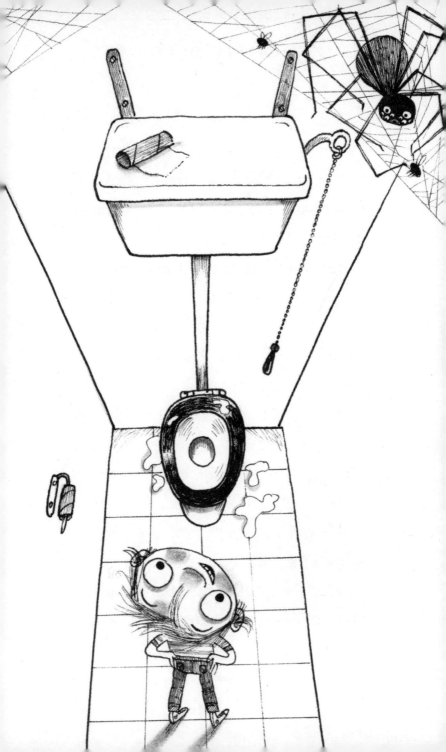

On the package: *For Bertie Love from Gran x*

CHAPTER 1

Bertie's gran often dropped round
for tea in the afternoon. Today she'd
brought along a large package wrapped
in silver paper.

"What have you got there, Gran?"
asked Suzy.

"Actually, it's a little present for
Bertie," said Gran. "I know it's a bit late

for Christmas but I hope he likes it."

A *present?* Bertie didn't mind getting presents at any time of year! What could it be? Maybe the Worm Farm he'd been saving up to buy or the Super Stinker Stinkbomb Kit his parents had refused to get him. He tore off the wrapping.

"A jumper," he said flatly.

"I knitted it myself," Gran smiled.

Bertie could have guessed that by the number of holes in it. He held up the huge baggy jumper, which was the colour of school custard. A row of fluffy white lambs skipped across the front. Bertie thought it was probably the worst jumper in the history of jumpers.

"Aww, isn't that lovely?" cooed Mum. "What do you say, Bertie?"

"Um, thanks, Gran," mumbled Bertie.

"Try it on!" cried Suzy eagerly.

Bertie glared at his sister — she was obviously enjoying this. Reluctantly, he pulled it on. The sleeves dangled down and it hung to his knees. It was more like a dress than a jumper!

"It's too big!" he protested.

"Nonsense, you'll soon grow into it," said Mum.

"It's meant to be big, that's the style

these days!" beamed Gran.

"And the little lambs are *so* sweet,"
grinned Suzy. "Why don't you wear it to
school tomorrow?"

Wear it to school? You must be joking!
thought Bertie.

"I'm not allowed to wear jumpers," he
said. "It's against the rules."

"Don't be silly," said Mum. "You often
wear a jumper to school."

"But not like this, mine are all brown!"
said Bertie.

"Then it will make a nice change," said
Suzy. "I bet none of your friends has got
a jumper like that."

Bertie was certain they hadn't. They
wouldn't be seen dead in a custard-
yellow jumper with skipping lambs on
the front.

Dirty Bertie

"Well, it's very kind of you, Gran," said Mum.

"Oh, it's no trouble at all," laughed Gran. "I love knitting. I could knit one for you if you like, Suzy?"

"Yes! Great idea!" cried Bertie.

"Oh no, that's okay, Gran," said Suzy quickly. "Wool makes me itchy. But I'm looking forward to Bertie wearing his new jumper to school."

Dirty Bertie

Bertie scowled. There was no way he was wearing the knitted horror to school. His friends would never stop laughing. Miss Boot would probably make him stand up in assembly to show the whole school! No, there was only one thing for it – he'd have to hide the jumper somewhere no one could find it.

CHAPTER 2

The next morning, Bertie got dressed for school. He pulled on his pants, jeans and T-shirt. He opened the bottom drawer where he kept all his jumpers.

HELP! *Where had they all gone?* The drawer was empty! He rushed downstairs in a panic.

45

Dirty Bertie

"Mum, where are all my jumpers?" he asked.

"Oh, they were dirty, so I put them in the wash," said Mum with a knowing smile.

"*ALL of them?*" cried Bertie. "But what am I going to wear to school?"

"Your new jumper of course," said Mum. "I found it under your bed. I can't think how it got there."

Dirty Bertie

"I can't wear that!" moaned Bertie. "It's too big! It looks like a dress!"

"Don't be silly," said Mum. "Anyway, you promised Gran you'd wear it today."

Bertie didn't remember promising anything. This was so unfair!

He thumped back upstairs. It was a plot. His mum had washed all his other jumpers on purpose.

Five minutes later he was back. Mum looked up.

"Bertie!" she said. "You can't go to school in just a T-shirt."

"Why not?" asked Bertie.

"Because it's winter, you'll freeze to death!" said Mum.

"I can run around!" said Bertie. "I'll be fine."

"I'm not arguing with you," said Mum.

Dirty Bertie

"You're wearing the nice jumper Gran knitted and that's the end of it. Go and put it on."

Bertie trailed down the road to school. He was wearing the knitted horror but at least nobody could see it. He had his coat zipped up to his neck.

Eugene and Darren were waiting on the corner as usual.

"Hi, Bertie!" said Eugene. "What's that yellow thing?"

Bertie looked down. Help! The jumper was so long it was sticking out below his coat! He tried to tuck it in.

"Are you wearing a nappy?" asked Darren.

"Very funny," said Bertie. "If you must

Dirty Bertie

know it's a jumper my gran knitted."

"Oh! A Granny jumper!" Darren
smiled.

"Well, let's see it then," said Eugene.

Dirty Bertie

"Yes, show us," urged Darren. "We won't laugh, will we, Eugene?"

Bertie sighed and fingered the zip on his coat. Should he? No, he couldn't face it.

"Is that the time? We'll be late for school," he said, hurrying on.

The others raced after him.

"Come on, Bertie, you can't keep your coat on all day!" said Darren.

Oh no? You just watch me, thought Bertie.

In the playground, Bertie stood with his friends, keeping his coat firmly zipped up. When the bell went they all filed into school. Bertie's classmates hung up their coats. Bertie kept his on. He sneaked into class and sat down at the back. Miss Boot was taking the register.

Dirty Bertie

"Donna?" she boomed.

"Yes, Miss!"

"Nicholas?"

"Here, Miss Boot!"

"BERTIE?" Miss Boot looked up. "Bertie, why are you still wearing your coat?"

Bertie turned pink. "The zip's stuck!" he said.

"Don't talk nonsense," barked Miss Boot. "Take it off!"

"I can't! It won't budge!" wailed Bertie, pretending to tug at the zip.

Miss Boot sighed. She marched over, grabbed the zip and yanked it down.

"There!"

By now the class had all turned round to stare. Bertie gulped and slipped off his coat. His classmates giggled.

Dirty Bertie

"Ooh, nice jumper, Bertie!" jeered Royston.

Dirty Bertie

"Ahh, it's so cute!" smirked Know-All Nick. "Look at the lickle lambies!"

Bertie glared at them. "If you must know, my gran knitted it," he said.

Miss Boot's mouth twitched.

"Don't listen to them, Bertie," she said. "I think it's very er … colourful."

This set off new waves of giggles. Bertie turned pink and slumped back in his seat. This was worse than the time he had to wear a kilt for his cousin's wedding. There was only one way to put an end to it – the knitted horror would have to go. But how could he get rid of it? Suddenly it came to him. It was Thursday – they went swimming on Thursday… What better place to lose a jumper than at the swimming baths?

CHAPTER 3

The coach pulled into the car park and everyone trooped off. Darren put on his swimming goggles.

"Your jumper's so bright it's hurting my eyes," he explained.

"Very funny," scowled Bertie. "Anyway, I won't be wearing it much longer."

"Oh, why's that then?" asked Eugene.

Dirty Bertie

"Yes, why *is* that?" sneered a voice.
It was Know-All Nick, his old enemy.

"Mind your own business, big nose,"
said Bertie.

Bertie waited until the swimming
lesson was over. Now was his chance.
He grabbed his clothes and slammed
the locker door shut, leaving the knitted
horror inside. By the time anyone found
it he'd be gone. He looked around. Only
Know-All Nick was about, combing his
hair in a mirror.

"All right, Bertie?" he smiled slyly.
"Sure you've got
everything?"

"Yes thanks," said Bertie.

Once he was dressed, he hurried to the coach and found a seat. He'd done it. *Goodbye, knitted horror!* he thought. *I won't be seeing you again!*

Mr Weakly climbed on to the coach with Know-All Nick. Bertie stared in disbelief. The teacher had something in his hand – a custard-yellow jumper.

"Has … ah … anyone lost a jumper?" he asked, holding it up.

Bertie slid down in his seat.

"Please, sir, I think it's Bertie's," Nick bleated. "He's always losing things!"

"Bertie, is this yours?" asked Mr Weakly.

"Oh yes, it's *definitely* his," said Darren.

"It's his favourite," added Eugene.

Bertie glared at them. So much for friends!

"Well, you better look after it," said
Mr Weakly. "You're lucky that Nicholas
found it. Aren't you going to thank
him?"

Bertie ground his teeth.

"Thanks *a lot*, Nickerless," he said.

"That's all right," smirked Nick. "I'd
hate you to lose your lovely new jumper.
I'll have to keep an eye on it for you!"

Dirty Bertie

The coach set off. Bertie glared at the jumper in his lap. Trust Know-All Nick to ruin everything, he thought. Why couldn't he mind his own business?

"Nice try, Bertie. Better luck next time," grinned Darren.

"It's all right for you," grumbled Bertie. "You don't have to wear it."

"It's not *that* bad," said Darren.

"All right, why don't we swap?" suggested Bertie. "I'll wear *your* jumper."

"No way!" snorted Darren. "I'm not wearing that thing."

Bertie stared out of the window. There had to be some way to get rid of the knitted horror. Suddenly it came to him. It was simple – all he had to do was leave it on the coach when he got off.

Ten minutes later, the coach pulled up

Dirty Bertie

outside the school. Bertie bent down
and quickly stuffed the jumper under
his seat. He joined the queue, anxious
to get off. Once the coach drove away
he'd be home and dry, free at last! He
jumped down the steps and hurried to
the gates.

"OH, BERTIE!" sang a voice
behind him. "Aren't you forgetting
something?"

Bertie swung round.
His heart sunk.
Know-All Nick was
waving the dreaded
jumper in the air.

"Noooo!"
moaned Bertie.
Was he never going
to get rid of it!

CHAPTER 4

For the rest of the day Bertie put up
with all the funny comments about his
jumper.

"HA HA! Look at Bertie!"

"Did you knit that yourself?"

"Is it a jumper or a dress?"

Bertie tried everything to get rid of it.
He left it in the cloakroom, the toilets

Dirty Bertie

and even in the lost property box. But the jumper always came back like a boomerang. Know-All Nick made it his personal mission to make sure he found it. In desperation, Bertie tried to throw the jumper into a tree, but he missed and it flopped down, landing on Miss Boot's head. At the end of the day Bertie plodded home with his friends. "Cheer up, Bertie," said Eugene. "I bet everyone will have forgotten it by tomorrow."

"Not if my mum makes me wear it again," moaned Bertie. "It's so big I'll still

61

be wearing it when I'm eighteen!"

"Hey, Bertie, catch!"

A ball whizzed past his head, bounced off a lamppost and shot over a fence.

Darren threw up his hands. "That's my super bouncy ball! Why didn't you catch it?" he grumbled.

"It's not my fault," replied Bertie. "I wasn't even looking!"

They peered over a tall wooden fence into a front garden. The ball lay in the middle of the lawn.

"We could climb over and get it," suggested Eugene.

"Darren could," said Bertie. "It's *his* ball."

"I'm not going! You're the one who lost it," argued Darren.

Bertie sighed and took off his coat.

Darren gave him a leg up and helped

Dirty Bertie

him climb over the fence. Getting the ball was the easy part – getting back proved more difficult. Bertie had to jump and hang on while trying to haul himself up. Eventually he managed to get one leg over the fence. That was when something got caught.

"AAARGH! I'm stuck!" he wailed.

"Hurry up, I think someone's coming!" warned Eugene.

Dirty Bertie

Bertie gave one last tug and managed to pull himself free. He jumped down, almost landing on top of Darren.

Eugene pointed. "Oh no, look what you've done!"

Bertie looked down. A thread of wool hung loose from the bottom of his jumper. It must have caught on the fence! He shrugged his shoulders. It was too late to do anything about it now.

Back home, Bertie walked in and dumped his coat on the floor. His mum was in the kitchen having tea with Gran.

"Here he is!" cried Gran. "And look, he's wearing his lovely new— Oh dear!"

She broke off. Mum raised a hand to her head.

Dirty Bertie

"What?" said Bertie. "What's wrong?"

Looking down, he saw that the knitted jumper had shrunk. In fact most of the bottom half was gone, leaving only the lambs' jolly faces. A long thread of wool led back down the hallway and out of the door. It must have unravelled on the way home!

Dirty Bertie

"Oops! Sorry, Gran," mumbled Bertie.

Mum shook her head in despair. "Really, how do you manage it, Bertie? You only wore it for one day!"

One day was quite enough, thought Bertie. He tried to look sorry but inside he felt like dancing. Yahoo! He'd got rid of it! He'd never have to wear the knitted horror again!

"Oh well, these things happen," sighed Gran. "Luckily for you I've just seen the perfect thing in my magazine – a rainbow jumper with darling little bunnies."

Bertie turned pale.

"Aww! I'm sure he'll love it," cooed Mum. "What do you say to Gran, Bertie?"

CHAPTER 1

Bertie and his friends were on the way back from their Saturday trip to the sweet shop.

"You won't believe what my dad's just bought," said Eugene.

"A speed boat," said Bertie.

"Even better than that," said Eugene. "A metal detector!"

Dirty Bertie

Bertie and Darren stared.

"A metal *detective*?" said Darren.

"No, a *detector*," repeated Eugene. "It's a machine which finds stuff buried in the ground."

"Like dead bodies, you mean?" said Bertie.

"No! Metal stuff like spoons or rings," explained Eugene. "If you're really lucky you might even find gold!"

"GOLD?" Bertie almost choked on his jelly snake.

"Well, obviously not all the time," admitted Eugene. "So far we've only found a sardine tin and an old dog tag. But my dad says a man once dug up treasure worth millions. It was sitting in a field for hundreds of years and nobody knew."

Bertie's eyes shone. This
was fantastic! He'd always
dreamed of finding buried
treasure and here was his
big chance!

"Well, what are
we waiting for?" he cried.

"You think there's gold buried round
here?" asked Darren.

"I don't see why not, there are loads
of fields," replied Bertie. "And if we've
got your detective machine we're bound
to find it."

"It's not mine though, it's my dad's,"
Eugene reminded them. "And he doesn't
like me using it without him."

Dirty Bertie

"But we only need it for a few hours," said Bertie.

"Yes, and you don't have to tell him we borrowed it," said Darren.

"Hmm," said Eugene doubtfully. "Well, I suppose not."

They waited while Eugene ran home to fetch the metal detector. Bertie couldn't think why his parents hadn't bought their own machine. Didn't they *know* you could find actual GOLD buried in the ground?

Soon Eugene was back. The metal detector looked like a space-age walking stick. It had a metal ring at one end, and a screen with a dial.

"That's it?" said Bertie.

"I thought it would be more like a giant digger," said Darren.

Eugene looked anxious. "I have to get it back by this afternoon," he warned. "If my dad finds out we've borrowed it, he'll go up the wall."

"That gives us plenty of time," said Bertie. "Let's try it in my back garden."

Bertie's mum was working at the kitchen table.

"Hello," she said. "And where are you three off to?"

"Just to play in the garden," answered Bertie. "We're hunting for buried treasure."

"Oh, I see," smiled Mum. "And what's

that you've got, Eugene?"

"It's a metal detector – we're, er …
borrowing it from my dad," said Eugene.

"It'll show us if there's gold in the back
garden," explained Bertie.

Mum raised her eyebrows. "Well,
good luck with that," she said. "Just
make sure you don't tread on any of
my plants."

"We won't!" Bertie promised.

He hurried outside. Who cared about
a few droopy old plants? If they found
gold they'd be able to buy a palace with
its own garden, swimming pool and
even a helicopter pad!

CHAPTER 2

The treasure hunters decided to start on the back lawn.

"I should go first, because it's my garden," said Bertie.

"Yes, but it's my metal detector," argued Eugene.

"What about me? When do I get a turn?" grumbled Darren.

Dirty Bertie

In the end Eugene went first as he was the only one who knew how to make the metal detector work. Bertie thought it looked pretty simple – you just pointed it at the ground and if it beeped and went crazy you'd found gold.

Eugene clicked a button and moved the metal ring from side to side as the machine hummed and ticked.

"Anything?" asked Bertie.

"Give me a chance," said Eugene. "If it finds anything it makes a noise and the needle on the dial jumps about."

Bertie moved in closer, watching the needle for the faintest movement. They reached the bottom of the lawn without a beep from the machine then turned around.

"Let me try," said Bertie, grabbing it.

Dirty Bertie

"Maybe you're not doing it right."

"I am!" said Eugene. "You just have to give it time."

Bertie strode up the lawn, waving the detector around like a magic wand.

"You're doing it too fast!" cried Eugene. "You have to take it—"

BEEP! BEEP! BEEP!

Bertie stopped dead. The needle had shot up the dial. This was it! They'd found gold!

"Quick, get a spade!" he cried.

Darren found a spade in the shed and started to dig.

"WAIT!" shouted Bertie.

He bent down and picked something out of the mud. It was a dirty toy car missing a wheel.

Dirty Bertie

"I wondered where that had got to," said Bertie.

"Huh! So much for finding gold!" sighed Darren.

"I told you it picks up anything that's metal," said Eugene. "You're not going to find gold coins every single time."

For the next half an hour, they combed the lawn from top to bottom. At last they sat down to inspect their finds. There was a swimming badge, a rusty screw, a toy car and a penny. It wasn't exactly the treasure Bertie had in mind.

Dirty Bertie

"Maybe we're not looking in the right place," he sighed.

"My dad says it's all about knowing where to search," agreed Eugene. "For instance, in the old days the Romans probably lived around here."

"What? In Bertie's house?" said Darren.

"No! But sometimes people find bits of Roman pottery in their gardens," said Eugene. "I've seen them in Pudsley museum."

"Well, if they've found pottery, I bet there's gold buried somewhere," said Bertie.

He'd been hoping for pirate treasure but Roman gold was even better! There might be gold cups, helmets, swords and daggers studded with jewels. Maybe they'd find a Roman money box stuffed with gold coins! Think how much that would be worth – millions or possibly billions.

"I know, let's look in the park," Bertie suggested.

"Why the park?" asked Eugene.

"Why not? The Romans must have had parks," Bertie argued.

"Yes, but thousands of years ago it probably wasn't a park," Eugene pointed out. "It could have been the Roman baths!"

"Even better," said Bertie. "People are always leaving stuff at the baths."

"Hang on, though," said Darren. "You can't go digging up the park."

"Why not?" asked Bertie. "It's only grass. Who's going to care about a few little holes?"

Dirty Bertie

Speaking of holes, he noticed that the back lawn had quite a few. Small piles of earth lay heaped everywhere you looked. Mum wasn't going to be too pleased about that. Maybe a trip to the park was a good idea!

CHAPTER 3

The park was busy with people. Whiffer had tagged along, despite Bertie ordering him to go home. He was now bounding around getting in everyone's way. The treasure hunters looked around.

"This is no good," said Eugene. "We'll never find anything with all these people."

Dirty Bertie

"HEY YOU!"

A man in uniform was marching towards them. Bertie groaned. Mr Monk lived on his street and was always complaining. Now he was a park-keeper he had a lot more to complain about, such as litter, dog poo and children enjoying themselves.

"Is that your dog?" he demanded. "I've just seen him digging in the sandpit."

"Sorry, Mr Monk," mumbled Bertie.

The park-keeper folded his arms. "And what are you three up to?"

"Nothing," replied Bertie.

Mr Monk pointed a finger. "Is that a metal detector?"

"Um, yes … it's my dad's. We're borrowing it," admitted Eugene.

Dirty Bertie

"Humph," said Mr Monk. "Well, you can't use it here. Metal detectors aren't allowed in the park."

"We're not using it," explained Bertie. "We're just looking after it."

"Is that right?" frowned Mr Monk. "Well, you better behave. I've got my eye on you and don't forget it."

Dirty Bertie

He stomped off back to his weeding.

"Maybe we should look somewhere else," suggested Eugene.

"I don't see why," said Bertie. "It's our park as much as his."

"Yes, but you heard him, metal detectors aren't allowed," said Darren. "We can't go digging up the grass."

"We're not digging up anything," said Bertie. "We're just going for a little walk. Come on."

They walked on until they were out of sight. Bertie switched on the metal detector and it hummed into life.

The park turned out to be the perfect place to find treasure – but only if you wanted bottle caps, ring pulls or drink cans. After an hour of poking around among the trees, Darren and Eugene had had enough.

"Let's go home," moaned Darren. "We're never going to find any gold."

"At least we found 2p, it's better than nothing," said Eugene.

But Bertie wasn't beaten yet. If someone had found Roman gold in a field why couldn't they find it in the park?

"One last try," he begged. "We haven't looked over there yet."

He pointed to a flower bed full of Mr Monk's prize roses.

"Bertie! We can't!" said Eugene. "What if Mr Monk comes back?"

Bertie looked around. "He's not here," he said. "He's probably gone home for lunch. Anyway it'll only take a minute!"

They crept in among the rose bushes.

Dirty Bertie

"POOH! It stinks!" cried Darren, stepping in some compost.

"Hurry up, Bertie, before he comes," said Eugene.

Bertie swept the metal detector over the earth. Nothing. He walked forward…

BEEP! BEEP! BEEP!

"I've got something!" he cried.

The needle on the dial was going crazy. Bertie got down on his hands and knees, digging with the spade they'd brought. It didn't take long before he found it – a single coin shining silver in the dirt.

"Look!" cried Bertie, grabbing it. This was it – they'd struck gold – or silver at least.

They crowded round to examine the coin. It looked old, although it was hard to tell because it was covered in dirt.

"Let's take it back to your house and clean it up," suggested Eugene.

Just then Whiffer came racing up and barked. Bertie looked round. Mr Monk was charging down the path like an angry bull.

"OI! GET AWAY FROM MY ROSES!" he roared.

"Uh-oh," said Bertie. Faced with a hopping-mad Mr Monk there was only one thing to do – run for their lives.

CHAPTER 4

On Bertie's road, they stopped to get their breath back. Mr Monk had chased them to the park gates but seemed to have given up.

"That was terrible!" panted Eugene. "What if he tells our parents?"

"Never mind that," said Darren. "Have you still got the coin, Bertie?"

Dirty Bertie

Bertie pulled it from his pocket and wiped it on his trousers.

It smelled pongy but it wasn't like any coin he'd seen before. It was silver with writing around the edge.

"I bet you it's Roman," said Bertie. "It's even got the king's head on it."

"The Romans had emperors," Eugene pointed out.

"Well, the emperor's head, then. It must be worth loads," said Bertie. "Maybe two or three million."

Wait till they heard about this at school, he thought. Miss Boot would be amazed.

Dirty Bertie

She'd probably ask him to give a talk about the Romans in assembly. They'd get their picture in all the papers. They'd probably get their own TV show. Bertie tossed the coin high into the air...

OOOPS! The coin slipped through his fingers, hit the pavement and rolled away. It vanished down a drain with a plop!

There was a stunned silence.

"You idiot, Bertie!" groaned Darren. "What did you do that for?"

"I didn't mean to," cried Bertie. "I meant to catch it!"

He got down on his hands and knees and peered into the drain. He could see the coin, shining silver among the mucky gunk and leaves. He tried to wriggle his hand through the bars of the drain but the gap was too narrow.

"I don't believe it," grumbled Darren. "At last we find a Roman coin and you chuck it away!"

"It was an accident!" said Bertie. "There must be some way to get it back."

"There is one thing we could try," said Eugene. "Wait here!"

Dirty Bertie

Ten minutes later, Bertie and Darren watched as Eugene lowered a piece of string down into the drain. Tied to the end was a super strong magnet. Eugene fished around. It took a few attempts but finally he pulled the string slowly back up. The silver coin was stuck to the magnet, caked in mud. Bertie grabbed it before it fell. Yes! They were back in business.

In the kitchen, Bertie's mum was making lunch.

"You'll never guess what we found!" cried Bertie, running in.

"Don't tell me – buried treasure,"

said Mum.

"Yes! A Roman coin!" said Bertie, holding it up. "It's real silver and millions of years old!"

Mum took it from him. "A Roman coin, hmm? Let's have a look at it," she said.

Going over to the sink, she washed off all the mud and held the coin up to the light.

"Ah, that's interesting," she said. "I wonder where it came from."

Dirty Bertie

"Is it Roman?" asked Bertie hopefully.

"Hardly," laughed Mum. "It's Canadian. Look, it says there, fifty cents."

"WHAT?" cried Bertie.

After all they'd been through to rescue the coin, it turned out it wasn't Roman at all! The treasure hunters looked at each other. Bertie's shoulders drooped.

"You mean it's not worth millions?" he asked.

"I doubt it," said Mum. "Maybe around 10p. Still, I'll look after it while you finish your jobs."

"Jobs?" said Bertie. "What jobs?"

Mum steered him to the window.

"It looks like someone dug up half the lawn," she said. "I'd like all those holes filled in, please. Now."

Dirty Bertie

Bertie rolled his eyes. It was the last time they borrowed a metal detector. The only thing they'd found all day was heaps of trouble!

MALPAS
28/3/19